Oliver's Ghost

Oliver's Ghost

A Spooky Tale from Nantucket

by Warren Hussey Bouton

Illustrated by Barbara Kauffmann Locke

Hither Creek Press
Short Hills, New Jersey

*This book is dedicated to
Bob Bouton and to all
loved ones past and present.*

CHAPTER

1

"For heaven's sake, Sarah, will you please be quiet for a minute so that I can tell one of *my* stories?"

"Oh come on, Ben, what have you got to talk about anyway besides silly baseball games and yucky *boy* stuff?"

"It's a lot more interesting than listening to you blabber on and on about all your singing, acting, and silly *girl* stuff," I responded with a huff.

Sarah had been talking constantly from the moment we sat down to dinner with my grandparents. Of course, I was kind of used to hearing her talk, but after all, we hadn't seen Grandma and Grandpa since the summer before, and I wanted to fill them in on what I'd been doing, too.

It was great to be back on Nantucket again. It felt as if we had been coming here for summer vacation forever and ever. Sometimes we came with my parents and stayed at the family cottage in Madaket. Other years, when Mom and Dad couldn't get away from work, my sister Sarah and I stayed with our grandparents in their house on Main Street. That's what we were doing again this year.

Grandma and Grandpa's house has been in the family for generations and is a big old creaky place with all kinds of spooky nooks and crannies. I always try to put on a good

front when we stay here, but to be honest, it scares me to death. Of course, the fact that the house seems to have more ghosts than live people has a lot to do with my fears. It feels as if every summer we run into some new spook that leads us into even scarier trouble than the year before. Sarah and I were determined this year to have a simple, fun-filled, ghost-free vacation.

"Now what in the world is that?" Grandma asked as she jumped up from the dining-room table and walked to the window. "Oh, I know what's going on. It's one of those ghost tours. I don't know why people pay good money to walk around Nantucket and listen to somebody go on and on about foolish ghosts that are supposed to be haunting the houses," she muttered disgustedly. "As far as I'm concerned, there are no such things as ghosts. Some people just let their imaginations run wild. There are no more ghosts in that house across the street than there are in this one!"

Sarah and I looked at each other with wide eyes. We knew there were plenty of ghosts on the island. After all, we'd met them not only at Grandma and Grandpa's house but at the cottage in Madaket, too. Unfortunately for us, we hadn't met them all…yet.

CHAPTER
2

Sarah and I just couldn't resist trying to hear what the ghost tour guide had to say, so we hustled out onto Grandma and Grandpa's front porch and plopped ourselves down to listen. The man, surrounded by about fifteen nervous-looking people, was pointing to the house across the street.

I had to admit that if there was ever a house that looked haunted, this one was it. The place was falling apart. Paint was peeling. Clapboards were falling off. The yard looked as if it hadn't been mowed in at least a hundred years. A chain with a sign that read "No Trespassing" ran across the driveway, and the path leading to the front door was blocked by an old gate that was covered with vines that had long since withered and died.

"No one has lived in this house for over fifty years," the tour guide explained. "The last owners were frightened away by strange and horrible happenings. They became so terrified that they finally packed up all their belongings and locked the door, never to return. Legend has it that when they left the island, instead of tossing pennies overboard at Brant Point in hopes of returning to Nantucket, they threw the key to this house into the water. The doors have been locked and the house has been empty ever since except, no doubt, for the ghosts that drove them away."

"What hogwash!" Grandma whispered as the tour group people oohed and ahhed. "He's right that nobody has lived there for fifty years or so…but ghosts, in that house…I don't think so."

As the tour group wandered away, I looked over at the rundown old house again and something caught my eye. There was the head of a boy peeking out over the front gate watching the ghost tour people as they ambled down the street. He looked really sad, as if he were lonely and wanted the people to stay and visit with him. Slowly he turned his head and looked over at Sarah and me sitting on the porch. When our eyes met and he realized that I was watching him, his eyes grew frightened and he quickly ducked down behind the gate.

"Sarah, did you see that? There's a boy

over there hiding behind that gate. I saw him peeking at us."

"Ben, you're seeing things," Sarah chuckled. "You heard Grandma—nobody has lived there for a long time. With all the talk about ghosts and terrible happenings, you're letting your imagination get away from you. Let's go inside. I want to try to beat Grandpa at a game of cribbage."

"Maybe you're right, Sarah," I said as we headed in. "Maybe…"

Little did we know then that we were about to begin one more spooky adventure.

CHAPTER

3

I stretched myself awake as the morning sun streamed through my bedroom window, telling me that it was going to be a bright, beautiful Nantucket day. After one of Grandma's great breakfasts, Sarah and I decided, with a lot of encouragement from Grandma, to go over to the First Congregational Church and climb up to the tower. "You'll be able to see all over the island on a day like this," Grandma had assured us.

And you know what? She was right. It felt like a long way up as we climbed the stairs, but when we finally reached the room with windows that let us look out in all directions. it sure was worth it.

"Look," I called out, "you can see all the way to Madaket!"

"And over here," Sarah piped up excitedly, "there's the harbor—look at all the boats. That's Coatue over there, and you can even see Great Point Lighthouse."

"This is incredible. I could stay up here all day!" I exclaimed.

It really was great being able to see all over the island. It was almost like being a bird or flying in an airplane. The view was super.

We stayed up in the tower for a long time looking out one window and then the next. We watched as one of the Steamship Authority's boats pulled into the harbor. Finally Sarah said, "Come on, Ben. It's time we started back to Grandma's."

"Okay, but instead of walking back the regular way, let's take some of the side streets and explore a little bit."

I love wandering down the back streets that weave their way around town. There is always something to see. People are constantly adding on new sections to their houses or replacing the wooden shingles. There are carpenters pounding and painters painting just about everywhere you turn. Once in a while you can watch a backhoe or a little bulldozer clearing land for a new foundation.

Somehow we managed to wind our way back around to the top of Main Street. I didn't really know where I was leading Sarah, but when I spotted Caton Circle I said, "See, I knew where we were all the time. I knew this is where we'd come out."

"Sure you did, oh great pathfinder," Sarah muttered. "Sure you did."

As we ran up the steps of Grandma and

Grandpa's house, I looked over at the spooky place across the street and much to my surprise I spotted the boy I'd seen last night peeking over the gate. This time he was wandering through the tall weeds in the yard with his eyes glued to the ground. Every so often he'd stop and push aside a broken branch or part of an overgrown bush. It was as if he were looking for something he'd lost.

"Sarah," I whispered. "Look over there—the boy I saw last night is in the yard."

"What do you think he's doing?" Sarah wondered aloud.

"I don't know, but it seems kind of strange to me."

A time was coming soon when we would discover just how strange it really was.

CHAPTER 4

Let's go say hi," I said as I quickly headed down the steps and across the street with Sarah scurrying to catch up.

Walking up to the front gate, I poked my head over and called out, "Hi there! My name is Ben and this is my sister Sarah. What's your name and what are you doing?"

The boy, still wandering the yard, stopped in his tracks and looked up with startled eyes. "My...my...my name is Oliver," he stuttered.

"Well, Oliver, it's nice to meet you.

What in the world are you doing over there? My grandmother says that nobody lives in this house, but there you are wandering around as if you owned the place."

Oliver slowly walked over toward the gate. "Well, I'm sure your grandmother is a wonderful lady, but I'm afraid she's made a mistake. This is my home."

"Your home?" I wondered aloud. "Well, it sure looks as if it has seen better days."

"Ben," Sarah whispered in my ear. "Do you think you could be a little nicer? It's not his fault the place is falling apart."

"You don't live here by yourself do you?" I questioned. "Are your parents here?"

"No…no. My parents are…away. But I don't live alone."

As Oliver said this he looked back quickly at the house as if he were afraid that someone or something might hear him talking to us.

Just as he looked back at us I thought I saw something move inside the house by one of the windows. Whatever it was, it was dark and moved slowly behind the curtain like a strange, heavy shadow.

"What was that?" Sarah asked.

"Nothing!" Oliver piped up. "I'm sure you're just seeing things. It was nothing. I've got to go now."

"I'm sure I saw something, too," I countered.

"NO! You didn't see anything!" Oliver cried.

Just then we heard Grandma's voice calling to us. "Sarah...Ben—it's time for you to be getting ready for lunch."

"We've got to go now, Oliver," Sarah said. "Maybe we'll see you tomorrow."

Oliver, looking sad, responded, "Maybe tomorrow."

As Sarah and I crossed the street and headed up Grandma and Grandpa's stairs I couldn't help looking back at the window where we had seen the strange dark shadow…and there it was again! But this time I had the scary feeling that not only was I looking at *it*, but *it* was looking at me.

CHAPTER
5

We ran into the kitchen just as Grandma was putting the makings of a massive lunch on the table. There were mounds of bread, cold cuts, chicken salad, leftover cold pizza, macaroni salad, and potato chips, not to mention a big plate of homemade chocolate chip cookies for dessert.

"Now let's get some lunch into you and then, once you've feasted on my cookies, we'll drop the two of you off at the beach. Which beach would you like to go to today?"

Sarah quickly answered without even

giving me a chance. "How about Jetties Beach? When we were up in the church tower there were all kinds of boats going in and out of the harbor. I'm sure there'll be a ton more this afternoon, and if we're at the Jetties they'll have to go right by us."

For once I really couldn't argue with Sarah's thinking. The Jetties was one of my favorite beaches and it was fun to watch the boats and the windsurfers.

"That's okay with me." I said. "But sometime while we're here I'd really like to go out to Madaket again."

"I'm sure that can be arranged, Benjamin," Grandpa said as he walked in the kitchen door. "Say, while I was in my workshop this morning I couldn't help noticing the two of you across the street. What were you doing over there?"

"We met a boy who says he lives there," I answered.

"Well that's funny," Grandpa said with a puzzled look, "because when I looked over I didn't see anybody except the two of you."

"And you say he claims to live there?" Grandma questioned. "I'm sure he must be pulling your leg, Ben. I've told you—nobody has lived there for years."

"Well, I can't help it, but that's what he said. Are you sure you didn't see him Grandpa? He was right there on the other side of the gate."

"Nope, I didn't see another soul. Who knows—maybe the two of you were talking to a ghost," Grandpa chuckled. "Maybe that man who runs the ghost tour is right and the house *is* haunted."

Grandma let out a loud laugh. "That'll be the day. Now Grandpa, don't go filling the children's heads with that kind of foolishness."

Sarah and I would have laughed along with Grandma, except both of our heads were already filled with the picture of that dark shadow moving behind the curtain.

CHAPTER
6

When lunch was over, Sarah and I ran upstairs, changed into our bathing suits, grabbed everything we needed for the afternoon, and then piled into the back of Grandpa's pickup truck. A ride in the truck was one of the things I really looked forward to every year. It just wasn't a summer vacation without feeling the wind blowing my hair and having my teeth rattled as Grandpa hit every bump in the road that he could find. The ride to the Jetties was a good one because Grandpa would always drive down a narrow little

cobblestone road as fast as he could. We would shake, bump, bounce, and laugh ourselves silly all the way down the hill. It was more fun than a ride at an amusement park.

Jetties Beach was great as usual. It was low tide and there were all kinds of families with little kids splashing in the shallow water between the sandbars. There were tons of people building sand castles, collecting shells, and swimming. Of course, what I liked best was watching people learn how to windsurf. They were constantly falling into the water, climbing back on board, and then as soon as the wind caught their sail, off they'd plunge again with a huge splash. Once in a while somebody was able to get the feel of balancing the sail pretty quickly and before you knew it they'd be flying over the water. That looked like fun!

After we'd walked the beach, built a sand castle, and had our fill of the windsurfers, Sarah decided to try to get our kite up in the air. Of course, she needed my help and before you could say Nantucket five times fast, I had that kite soaring in the breeze.

As we gazed up into the deep blue sky at the kite, Sarah said, "I wonder if Oliver would like to come to the beach with us?"

"I don't know," I answered, "I guess we could ask, but he doesn't look as if he knows how to have much fun. Did you see the way he kept looking back at the house?"

"Yeah. He seemed pretty scared about something."

"That's what I thought. And I don't care what he said, I saw something moving behind that window."

"So did I," Sarah replied as she gave the string holding our kite a quick tug.

"Whatever it was, Sarah, it was big, it was dark. It was somebody or something and it was watching every move we made and listening to every word we said."

"You don't think it was…a ghost…do you?"

"Who knows?" I answered slowly. "But something just doesn't seem right over there."

CHAPTER

7

The next morning, as we devoured huge plates of Grandma's fantastic French toast, Sarah and I agreed that we'd try to spot Oliver and invite him to the beach. We figured that if we could get him away from the house, maybe he'd tell us what was really going on over there.

We watched for him from the living room until Grandma came along and said, "What in the world are you two sitting around inside for? It's a beautiful day and you need to be outside. If you can't find something to keep yourselves occupied, I'm sure your Grandfather could use some help out in the shop, or I'll bet I could find a job for you myself."

When Grandma mentioned putting us to work, we knew we'd better scoot fast or Sarah and I would end up polishing silver or washing windows, so we headed for the door fast.

The front steps were a great place to keep an eye out for Oliver. It was also fun to watch the tourists as they rode by on their bicycles or stopped to check their maps. Even though we didn't live on Nantucket all the time, Sarah and I didn't consider ourselves tourists. We'd been coming to the island since before we could remember, and besides, my Dad's family went all the way back to the original settlers in 1659. There was no way anybody was going to call us tourists.

"Ben, there's Oliver," Sarah whispered. "He's starting to look for something in the yard again. I wonder what he's looking for?"

"How about we ask him? Hey, Oliver!" I shouted. "What are you looking for?"

We scampered down the stairs and across the street as Oliver looked up and smiled. Even though he still looked nervous, it was the first time he'd seemed happy to see us.

"Oliver, what in the world are you looking for?" I blurted out as we ran up to the gate.

"Something…something I lost a long time ago," Oliver whispered, looking quickly back at the house.

"Maybe we could help you look," Sarah offered.

"No…no, you mustn't come into the yard. It's something I have to find myself."

"Okay, if that's the way you feel about it. But you can't look all day. How about joining us for a little fun?" I asked. "Sarah and I were wondering if you'd like to go to the beach with us this afternoon."

Looking nervously back at the house, Oliver said in a hushed voice, "No…I can't do that."

"Well, would you like to go into town with us?" Sarah wondered. "We could walk around the docks and maybe check out the candy shop."

"It's not a good idea for me to leave," Oliver sighed. "He'll…he'll get mad."

"What do you mean he'll get mad? *Who'll* get mad?" I demanded.

"Never mind. Just go. For your own sake, leave me alone," Oliver moaned sadly.

"Oliver, we're worried about you. You seem lonely and scared about something. Don't you have anybody who can help you? Don't you have any family?" Sarah asked.

With that, Oliver looked up, gazed into our eyes, and said softly "Yes, you!"

As soon as the words were out of his mouth, Oliver started to fade away into a ghostly mist…and then he was gone.

CHAPTER
8

"Oh *noooo!*" Sarah groaned. "Not Oliver!"

"I can't believe this is happening," I muttered. "Why can't we come to Nantucket and just enjoy ourselves? Why do we keep running into spooks? Are we ghost magnets or what?"

This was turning into the fourth summer in a row that Sarah and I had suddenly found ourselves in the middle of a scary adventure. First we'd run into the ghost of a nasty old whaling captain named Ichabod Paddack. Then we'd nearly been burned to a crisp trying to help Cyrus, the ghost of one of our ancestors. And last year Paddack's ghost had showed up again nearly getting us swept out to sea in a rowboat—and if it hadn't been for another spook, Hannah Hussey, we'd probably still be floating out in the ocean somewhere between Nantucket and Spain!

"This is ridiculous," I fumed as I started stomping my way back to Grandma and Grandpa's house. "Who does he think he is? Getting us to feel sorry for him and then pulling his little disappearing act. I'm tired of ghosts. I'm sick of ghosts. I'm not interested in solving any more of their little problems. I've had it. I'm done!"

"Oh come on, Ben," Sarah begged. "He needs our help. He's scared of something."

"How can a ghost be scared of anything?" I cried. "He's already dead!"

"I don't know," Sarah admitted. "But I'm at least going to ask Grandma if there was ever somebody in our family named Oliver."

We found Grandma in the kitchen pantry making a shopping list for a trip to the grocery store.

"Grandma," Sarah asked. "Do we have any relatives named Oliver?"

"Oliver...Oliver..." Grandma pondered. "The only Oliver I can think of was...come on. Let's head up to the attic."

We followed Grandma up the steep stairs and down the hall to the back bedroom. The door to the attic that stood in the corner of the room had always been more than a little scary for Sarah and me. Whenever we stayed with my grandparents I tried to joke about it with Sarah, and more than once I'd hidden in the attic to scare her out of her wits by pretending to be a ghost, but even I got nervous when I walked through that door. Not Grandma! She plowed through the door and started rummaging around the attic, pulling sheets off of the family treasures that were stored there.

Finally, she called out, "Now we're getting somewhere. Come over here, children, and let's see if one of these old paintings might be what we're looking for. Yes, I think I've found it."

As Sarah and I inched our way to where Grandma stood, she pulled out a big old painting from a stack leaning against the chimney. When she turned, holding the painting for us to see, our jaws dropped. It was a portrait of Oliver!

"Now what's the matter with you children?" Grandma asked. "You look as if you've seen a ghost."

"No...uh Grandma," I stuttered as Sarah just stared at the picture. "It's just that he looks

like somebody we've… met."

"Well, I don't think you've met him. He would have been your great, great…oh I don't know how many greats, but he would have been a great-uncle of yours. I seem to remember hearing stories about him when I was growing up. As a boy he used to love being down on the waterfront. He rowed a rickety old boat around the docks and would crawl up the anchor chains on the whaling ships like a monkey. Someone once said that Oliver would climb up in the ship's rigging and lay out on the yardarms as if it were his own bed. He was a brave little boy who loved the sea and couldn't wait to go whaling. Unfortunately, he was washed overboard on his first voyage as a cabin boy."

"Where did the painting come from,

Grandma?" I asked.

"This painting used to hang in the house across the street. Oliver's parents owned it, but when Oliver was lost at sea they lost their love for the island and moved to the mainland."

With that, Grandma put the painting back in the stack and covered them all with a sheet again. "Come along, children. There's no sense in spending a beautiful day up here in a hot old attic. How about some lunch?"

"We'll be there in a minute, Grandma," I called out as she headed down the hall.

"Come on Sarah," I blurted as my sister gazed at the sheet covering the paintings. "Snap out of it!"

"I can't believe we've met another ghost," she finally said in a hushed voice.

"Yeah, well this one's going to get a

piece of my mind," I seethed. "I don't care who he is. I'm not falling for any more sad stories and ending up in trouble again."

"But he's lonely, Ben. And he's scared of something or someone in the house. What do you think Oliver meant when he said 'He'll get mad'?"

"I don't know, but whoever it is couldn't be madder than I am. I've got a lot of questions for *Uncle* Oliver and the next time I see him I'm going to get some answers!"

CHAPTER

9

I was still fuming after lunch. In fact, the more I stewed over the whole mess with Oliver, the madder I got. As Sarah and I sat on the front porch watching for Oliver I couldn't wait to let him have it!

I didn't have to wait long.

"There he is," I sputtered as Oliver walked around the corner of the house. "Let's go."

I stomped my way across the street, and Sarah and I squeezed through a hole in the hedge and walked right up to Oliver as he began his routine of searching the yard. When he looked up and saw us there in front of him he looked pretty startled.

"What are you doing here?" he whispered.

"What are *we* doing here? What are *you* doing here? Who do you think you are anyway *Uncle* Oliver? Why didn't you tell us that you were a ghost, and what are you looking for? You're probably just trying to lure us over here and make us feel sorry for you. Well, who cares? You can haunt this place from here to kingdom come if you want to. We've got better things to do."

As I shouted at Oliver, Sarah grabbed my arm and squeezed it, saying, "Ben I think you'd better stop now."

"What do you mean, stop? I'm just

getting warmed up."

"Ben, look at the window."

As soon as I looked up at the house I knew we were in trouble. The dark presence we'd seen at the window before was back, and it was getting darker and darker by the second. Suddenly it looked as if a huge wind had begun to blow in the house. The curtains were flapping like crazy, and then without any warning, the window shattered as the wind poured out of the house and swirled around us, almost like a tornado. Branches started to fall from the trees and that dark presence began floating toward us from the house.

"Now you've done it," Oliver shuddered, looking absolutely terrified.

The wind whipped around us so hard that it was almost impossible to catch a breath, and it became stronger as that dark presence came closer and closer. Finally, it stood right in front of me and spoke with a deep, haunting voice that made my knees shake: "Who are you to come into *my* yard and question *my* friend? Take your anger from this place or you will feel *my* wrath upon your face!"

"Let's get out of here!" Sarah screamed. She grabbed my arm again and dragged me toward the hedge. As we ran, the wind kept circling us and the dark presence laughed a spooky kind of laugh. We scrambled through the hedge as fast as we could and once we hit the street the wind stopped...but we didn't. Sarah and I scampered up the front steps as fast as we could and slammed the door, behind us. We were safe.

Collapsing on the floor with our backs to

the door Sarah and I slowly but surely caught our breath. When I could finally speak again, I blurted out, "What was that? Something really strange is going on over there."

Sarah shook her head. "It's not just strange, Ben. It's dangerous, and we're *not* going back."

CHAPTER 10

Sarah and I didn't talk much the rest of the day. I think we were both in shock from what had happened across the street. We even mumbled our way through dinner. Grandpa was talking about last night's Red Sox game and tried to tease me into a conversation about whether they would ever win a World Series again. But I just shrugged and pushed my food around my plate. Grandma attempted to question Sarah about her last school play and what she'd enjoyed most about it. But my sister simply tilted her head, thought for a minute, and answered, "I don't know." I'm sure Grandma and Grandpa noticed that something was bothering us, but luckily they didn't ask. I have no idea what we would have told them.

Sarah and I helped Grandma with the dishes and then, even though I played checkers with Grandpa a bunch of times, I just couldn't get the sound of the wind, the ghostly laughter, and the memory of that dark presence out of my head. I didn't want to have anything else to do with ghosts and neither did Sarah.

When it was finally time to go to bed we trudged up the stairs without a word. As Sarah headed to her room down the hall, I closed my door and got into my pajamas. I tried to read for a while but I kept reading the same paragraph over and over again. Finally, I turned out the light. But just because I was in bed didn't mean that I was able to get to sleep. My mind just wouldn't stop. It kept racing and racing with thoughts of Oliver, whaling ships, and dark shapes floating in the air. Even after I drifted off into a restless sleep I could still see Oliver's desperate face in my dreams as the wind took my breath away and tree branches crashed down all around us.

CHAPTER
11

A strange creaking sound startled me awake. When I finally got my eyes open and looked around the room to see where the noise was coming from, I wasn't sure whether I was still dreaming or if what I was seeing was real. The sound was coming from a rocking chair in the corner of the room. It was rocking, but nobody was sitting in it. As I stared in disbelief, Oliver's ghostly outline began to appear.

"Are you all right, Ben?" Oliver asked.

"I was afraid for you and Sarah yesterday afternoon. Gideon doesn't like it when people come into the yard. And he certainly doesn't like people yelling at me."

"Gideon," I said. "Is that the name of whatever it was that blew out the window, swooped through the yard like a tornado, and chased us away?"

"Yes, that was Gideon, all right." Oliver answered.

"Does he live there in the house with you?" I questioned. "Where did he come from? Has he always been so mean?"

"No, he hasn't always been as scary as he is now. We worked on the whaling ship together. And after…the storm…we both found ourselves at my parents' house across the street."

"The storm," I said quietly. "Is that when you...died?"

"Yes, Gideon and I both...drowned. It shouldn't have happened. We were having a quiet day. I was up in the crow's nest keeping an eye out for whales. I didn't see a single one, but I did see a huge black cloud on the horizon making its way toward the ship. I called down to the captain to warn him, but he didn't seem to think it was going to be a danger to us. Then, as the sky grew darker by the minute, the rain started. Lightening cracked and thunder boomed all around us. And finally, the wind hit us from the side, howling through our rigging. The wind was so strong against the sails that the ship started to roll over. Our yardarms were skimming the waves. I hung onto the mast with all my strength, but then a wave hit me and I couldn't hold on any longer. The last thing I saw was the ship in the distance, righting itself and sailing on. Another wave washed over me and the next thing I knew...I was in my parents' yard and Gideon was there too."

Hearing Oliver's story, I couldn't help but feel sorry for him and even for Gideon. "But why is Gideon so mean?"

"He didn't start out that way," Oliver answered. "At first we got along pretty well. But then, Gideon started playing little tricks on my family. Like moving things, opening and closing doors to scare them. After my folks moved away and other people came to live in the house, Gideon began to do things that were really scary, even to me. He just became more and more angry. Finally, it got so bad that nobody wanted to live in the house anymore.

Then he started picking on me. I used to be so brave, climbing the ship's rigging, unfurling the sails, standing up for myself with the rest of the crew. But now Gideon gets so angry I'm afraid all the time. I never get a moment's peace. I know I should be strong and tell him to stop, but he bullies me. There's something evil about Gideon now. I'd like to get him to leave, but I'm afraid of what he might do to me and now…to you. I know I shouldn't ask, but can you help me?"

"I don't know, Oliver," I said shaking my head. "Can't you leave and get away from him?"

"I wish I could, but I know I've lost something, something important to me. That's why I wander around in the yard so much. Something's missing. I don't know what it is, but I can't leave until I find it. I won't get any peace until I find it."

I didn't say anything for a long time, but then I looked into Oliver's eyes and said, "I'm sorry. I don't know what Sarah and I can do. We're just kids and we're scared. Gideon is one mean ghost. I wish we could help you, but this is more than we can handle. We're not coming over today. Sarah and I are going on a bike ride. I'll talk to my sister, but don't expect any miracles."

Oliver looked really sad, but then he said, "I don't expect any miracles. But I am part of your family and I *know* you can help me *if*…you want to."

CHAPTER

12

"Whose idea was it to ride our bikes to 'Sconset anyway?" I muttered as we stopped to stretch our legs on a hill overlooking the little village that sits at the eastern end of Nantucket.

"Oh come on, Ben," Sarah answered, "You're the one who claims to be such a great athlete. Don't tell me that a little seven-mile bike ride is too much for you."

"Seven miles!" I sputtered. "That's only half of it. Don't forget we have to pedal all the way back!"

The ride really hadn't been too bad. We

had pedaled past the windmill, the hospital, and the high school. Then Sarah had suggested that we stop to get a drink at a snack shop by the rotary before we started the long stretch on the bike path. As we made our way out Milestone Road we saw lots of people on their bikes, not to mention folks on roller-blades, all making

the same trip. The time passed pretty quickly because there was a lot of traffic and always something to see.

As we looked down the hill toward 'Sconset I decided it was time to tell Sarah about Oliver asking for help.

"You've got to be kidding!" Sarah blustered. "How are we supposed to help him?"

"I don't know, Sarah," I responded. "But I've been thinking about it a lot. Remember a couple of years ago when I had that bully picking on me at school? It was horrible. Just like Oliver, I was scared all the time. When it finally got so bad that I couldn't stand it anymore I asked my teacher for help. I didn't know if she could do anything, but just talking about it made me feel better. And then before I knew it that bully was in the principal's office

58

and he never bothered me again."

"But Ben, there's no teacher who we can tell about Oliver. There's no principal in the world who's going to call Gideon into the office and give him detention. We're talking about ghosts here!"

"I know," I mumbled as I got on my bike. "But Oliver is family. He's being bullied just like I was and I'm going to help."

I pushed off and started pedaling as fast as I could down the hill. I honestly didn't know what I could do to help Oliver. But I knew I had to do something. I just had to.

CHAPTER
13

As we rode around 'Sconset I couldn't get Oliver out of my mind. I knew what he was feeling and I really wanted to help him. But how could I ever stop Gideon from being so mean? I could tell Sarah was thinking about it too, because instead of her usual running commentary on everything we were seeing—from the rose-covered cottages to the view of Sankaty Head Lighthouse off in the distance—she was as quiet as a mouse.

As we meandered around the tiny little streets, Sarah spotted some kids coming out of an artist's gallery and piped up, "Hey, Ben, let's stop for a minute and go in there."

"Give me a break, Sarah. Why in the world would I want to go look at paintings?"

"Because we rode our bikes all the way out here and we might as well see everything we can. Who knows—maybe a little culture will do you good and get your mind off Oliver."

We parked our bikes on a bike rack near the front door to the gallery and I trudged in behind Sarah. I have to admit that the paintings were pretty cool. The artist, who was sitting at a desk in the corner working on a small watercolor, obviously liked seagulls. Paintings of them were everywhere. They were kind of whimsical and fun. She even had tee shirts with seagulls in all kinds of different poses. There were other paintings too, of course, along with books that she had illustrated. But even though I was having a good time looking at all her stuff, I guess she could tell there was something really serious bothering me because as our eyes met she said, "It looks to me as if you're upset about something young man. Are

you all right?"

"I'm okay," I muttered as I tried to figure out a way to tell this lady about Oliver without saying that he was a ghost. "But a...a...friend...that's it, a friend...is in big trouble and I'm worried about him. You see, there's a bully who just won't leave him alone."

"A bully," the artist said with concern. "That is a problem. I know how scary that can be. Is there a chance that your friend can stay away from this bully?"

Sarah said, "No. Our...friend...can't stay away from him. You see, Oliver—that's our friend's name—has lost something important and this bully knows where he's searching. It's really kind of complicated. But this bully won't give Oliver a minute's peace."

The lady was quiet for a minute, glancing down at her work but then she looked into our eyes and said, "It sounds to me as if your friend Oliver needs to stand up to that bully. I think the first thing he needs to find is some courage."

"You may be right, ma'am," I answered. "But how in the world can we ever help him find courage?"

"Maybe Oliver just needs to know that the two of you care about him and believe in him. It's hard for someone to stand up to a bully alone. But if you're there with him, then maybe, just maybe, he'll find the strength he needs to put that bully in his place."

The artist's words brought butterflies to my stomach and I could see Sarah's knees start to shake. Could we really help Oliver stand up to Gideon? At that moment I just didn't know, but whether Sarah and I liked it or not, we would soon find out.

CHAPTER
14

As Sarah and I slowly pushed our bikes up Grandma and Grandpa's driveway we couldn't help but notice that there were dark clouds gathering, and they seemed to be centered over the house across the street.

"I don't think I can take another step," Sarah moaned as she plopped herself down on the grass of the back yard after parking her bike.

I collapsed beside her and stared up at the brewing storm as the wind started to build and rattle the tree branches.

"Do you think this weather has anything to do with Oliver and Gideon?" I wondered aloud.

"Oh please, Ben, not now! Can't we rest a little before you start playing the hero? I'm exhausted. Oliver has been living with Gideon's bullying for years. One more day isn't going to hurt."

"That's where you're wrong, Sarah. Oliver needs our help and he needs it now. You may not know what it's like to live with a bully, but I do, and a single day feels like forever."

"Ben, what are we going to do? Gideon is a ghost! Do you hear me—a ghost! G—H—O—S—T! How are we going to stop him?"

The wind really started to wail. It had a

haunting sound that made the hair on the back of my neck stand on end. I just knew something horrible was happening across the street. I could feel it in my bones. Oliver was in trouble and Sarah and I were the only people in the world who could help.

"Sarah, I'm going. You can stay here moaning and groaning about how tired you are. You can go hide under your bed if you're too scared to lift a finger to help Oliver. But I'm not going to stand by while a bully picks on somebody from my family. Ghost or no ghost, I'm going to help if it's the last thing I do!"

Sarah slowly pushed herself up off the ground and got to her feet. "Okay, Mr. Hero. I'll come too. But I sure hope it's *not* the last thing we ever do!"

CHAPTER
15

There was no sign of Oliver as Sarah and I ran across the street and squeezed through the hole in the hedge. We scampered through the yard, dodging countless tree branches that were falling to the ground. The wind was even stronger now and the two of us had a hard time keeping our balance.

When we reached the side of the house I scanned the yard one more time. "I guess if we want to find Oliver we're going to have to go inside," I whispered.

"Are you nuts?" Sarah almost screamed.

Her eyes grew wide with fear. "Gideon went crazy when he found us in the yard. What do you think he'll do if he sees us in the house?"

"We can't worry about that, Sarah. We're here to help Oliver and if Oliver is inside, that's where we're going."

We inched along the side of the house, fighting the wind all the way until we finally came to the window that Gideon had broken the day before.

"Give me a ten-finger boost, Sarah," I shouted against the wind. "Once I'm in I'll reach out and give you a hand."

"This is one of the dumbest things we've ever done," Sarah grunted as she leaned her back against the wall and boosted me through the open window.

It didn't take long to scramble through

and I quickly pulled Sarah in behind me. The room we were standing in was completely empty except for a lot of cobwebs and a ton of plaster that had fallen from the ceiling over the years. Every time we took a step the floors creaked, but it wasn't the creaking floor that caused our hearts to race; it was the noises that were coming from upstairs. We could hear Gideon's terrifying voice screaming, and it sounded as if furniture was being thrown against the walls. We crept toward a doorway that seemed to lead out into a hall and then suddenly there was silence.

"Someone's in my house!" Gideon shouted. "Who dares enter my house?"

Then instead of furniture smashing we heard footsteps. They grew louder and louder as they drew closer. We peeked around the corner of the doorway into the hall, and there on the stairs we saw Gideon's horrible dark presence making its way toward where Sarah and I were cowering.

"Maybe this wasn't such a good idea," I said with a quivering voice.

"Too late now, Mr. Hero," Sarah whimpered. "We came to save Oliver. Now who's going to save *us*?"

CHAPTER 16

"What are you doing in my house?" Gideon roared.

"We're…here…here to help Oliver," I stuttered.

"*Oliver!* Oliver doesn't need your help," Gideon sneered. "*Do* you, Oliver?"

It was then that we noticed Oliver standing on the stairs behind Gideon's angry, towering shape. Oliver looked sadder and more frightened than I had ever seen him.

"No…no I don't need any help," Oliver whispered. "Go home Sarah, and Ben. I never should have spoken to you."

"It's too late now," Gideon bellowed.

As he shouted, his form grew bigger and bigger, darker and darker. It seemed as if his body were made out of swirling black smoke that filled the entire stairway.

"Busybodies! Trespassers! I take care of Oliver," Gideon snarled. "And now I'll take care of you, too! *Wind of the east and wind of the west—seal my house as only you know best.*"

Before we knew what was happening, Sarah and I heard doors crashing closed and shutters slamming shut. The house grew dark, with only tiny streams of light seeping through the cracks of broken shutters.

Swirling winds suddenly began to twist Sarah and me around in circles as Gideon shouted, *"Spin, spin my nosy young friends. Ride my wind 'til time doth end. Let's hear you cry. Let's hear you grieve. You'll ride my wind for eternity!."*

Sarah and I were seized in what felt like a tornado. I grabbed at a door knob and managed to pull myself from the whirlwind but Sarah kept spinning around in what seemed to be a never-ending circle of wind, dust, and destruction. Plaster was spinning everywhere. Dust filled the air and I could hardly breathe. Broken glass from the window threatened to slash my sister and me at every turn. I hung on for dear life even as Sarah's hands reached out to try to grab anything that might save her from Gideon's grasp.

"Oliver! Do something!" I shouted. "Please! Do something!"

"What can I possibly do?" he shrieked. "It's Gideon. I have no power over Gideon."

"Oliver!" I shouted. "You have to save Sarah or she'll be lost forever."

I looked at Oliver as he stood there on the stairs. He hesitated. He was afraid and I knew that if he didn't act now, Sarah was lost forever.

CHAPTER
17

"Oliver! Please, DO something!" I pleaded. "Sarah needs you. She's family, Oliver. She's your family. Do you want to lose her to Gideon's anger? Do you want to see her swept away by his horrible wind?"

"No," Oliver whimpered.

"Then do something, NOW!"

Oliver took a deep breath. And then he breathed deeply again.

All of a sudden Gideon let out the most horrible laugh I have ever heard. He looked at Oliver and cried out, "Go ahead, my fearful little friend. Do something. I dare you!"

Oliver shook as he stared at Gideon and then looked at Sarah spinning around in the dizzying tornado.

It was now or never. "Oliver," I screamed as I suddenly remembered the artist's words. "I know what you lost. You lost your *courage*. FIND IT NOW! Sarah *needs* you. You were brave once. You told me so. Gideon is a ghost, but so are you! You can stop him! Stop him now! FIND YOUR COURAGE NOW!"

Oliver seemed shaken. He closed his eyes and took a deep breath. He breathed again and again, faster and faster. As he breathed something strange and wonderful began to happen. Oliver got bigger and bigger and bigger, and as he grew in size a beautiful light began to radiate from him. The light became brighter and brighter. Oliver opened his eyes and stared straight at Gideon and said, "I *was* brave once. I was *good* and *proud*. You have *no* right to frighten me. You have *no* right to hurt my family. I AM good, I CAN be brave. This...is...MY...house!"

I could hardly believe my eyes and ears. As Oliver spoke in his clear strong voice, he grew bigger and brighter and as he grew, Gideon's dark presence began to shrink. And as Gideon got smaller the tornado that had Sarah in its grasp began to slow. Gideon looked frightened now. He began to shake and his dark presence began to fade.

"You can't hurt me, Gideon," Oliver said with a strong voice. "You can't bully me or my family any more. I've had enough." And then he roared, "BE GONE!"

And in the blink of an eye, Gideon was gone. The wind stopped and Sarah dropped to the floor. I ran to my sister and as she caught her breath she looked up and gasped, "What happened? Where's Gideon?"

"It was Oliver," I said with a proud grin on my face. "He found his courage. That's what he lost so long ago—his courage."

I looked at Oliver and his smile filled the room. "You did it, Oliver!" I cried. "When you found your courage and Gideon saw your bravery, he did what most bullies do when someone is willing to stand up to them...he disappeared."

CHAPTER
18

"Sarah! Ben! Where in the world are you?" Grandma called from the front porch. "Time for dinner!"

We looked at Oliver and I said, "We've got to go, Oliver. Grandma's calling.

"I know," he answered. "When your Grandma has dinner on the table you'd better run."

"Will you be okay?" Sarah asked.

"Sarah, I'll be fine." Oliver said as his smile grew wider. "Gideon's gone. I'm free. I found what I was searching for—my courage—

and I was able to save you. I'm finally home again."

As Oliver spoke he slowly started to fade from sight until finally he disappeared.

"Where do you think he went?" Sarah wondered aloud.

"Sarah! Ben!" Grandma bellowed from across the street. "Dinner's ready! Get home now or you'll be going hungry tonight!"

"I don't know where Oliver went," I cried as the two of us started running for Grandma and Grandpa's house. "But I know where *we're* going if we want dinner."

Sarah and I ran across the street, up the stairs, through the front door, and jumped into our chairs at Grandma's dinner table as fast as our legs would carry us.

"So," Grandma questioned. "How was your day?"

Before we could even begin to answer we heard voices coming through the open windows from the street.

"Oh for heaven's sake," Grandma muttered with a disgusted voice. "There's that silly ghost tour again. You know, I'll bet I could tell them a ghost story or two that would really make their heads spin!"

Sarah and I looked at each other, shook our heads, and said together, "So could we, Grandma. So could we!"

Look for more spooky tales by

Warren Hussey Bouton

Sea Chest
in the Attic

The Ghost
on Main Street

The Ghost
of Ichabod Paddack

and

Oliver's
Ghost

For information about Hither Creek Press
or to contact the author send your email to:
Hithercreekpress@aol.com